P9-BBQ-294

I LOVE SCHOOL!

For Gina Shaw,
an editor and friend
without equal

No part of this publication may be reproduced, stored in
a retrieval system, or transmitted in any form or by any means, electronic,
mechanical, photocopying, recording, or otherwise, without written permission
of the publisher. For information regarding permission, write to Scholastic Inc.,
Attention: Permissions Department, 557 Broadway, New York, NY 10012.

ISBN-13: 978-0-545-13474-3
ISBN-10: 0-545-13474-9

Copyright © 2009 by Hans Wilhelm, Inc.

All rights reserved. Published by Scholastic Inc.
SCHOLASTIC, NOODLES, CARTWHEEL, and associated logos are
trademarks and/or registered trademarks of Scholastic Inc.
Lexile is a registered trademark of MetaMetrics, Inc.

12 11 10 9 8 7 6 5 4 3 2   9 10 11 12 13 14/0

Printed in the U.S.A.
First printing, September 2009

BEGINNING READER

LEVEL 1

50-250 WORDS

I LOVE SCHOOL!

by Hans Wilhelm

Cartwheel
·B·O·O·K·S·®

SCHOLASTIC INC.

New York   Toronto   London   Auckland   Sydney

Mexico City   New Delhi   Hong Kong   Buenos Aires

School looks like fun.

This must be the way inside.

What a big place!

Where is everyone?

Now I'm totally lost.

Ahhh!
What is *that*?

I have to get out of here!

I better stay out of the way.

This place is scary.
I feel all alone here.

Wait! That's silly!
School is not scary.
School is fun!

I can meet some
new friends.

Can I hear the story, too?

School is so much fun.
I am making lots of new friends.

The teacher is nice, too!

I think I'll come back tomorrow.